To my great family, remembering all our Christmases each year at various
Mackalls, Daleys, Pentos, Brigmons, McCarthys, Eberharts, Hendrens . . .
-DDM

For Glenn, Zachary, and Madison. Thanks for taking this wonderful trip with me—
from here to there and back again.
-MN

ZONDERKIDZ

17 Christmases
Copyright © 2010 by Dandi Daley Mackall
Illustrations © 2010 by Michele Noiset

Requests for information should be addressed to:

Zonderkidz, *Grand Rapids, Michigan 49530*

Library of Congress Cataloging-in-Publication Data

Mackall, Dandi Daley.
    17 Christmases / by Dandi Daley Mackall ; illustrated by Michele Noiset.
      p. cm.
    Summary: During the Christmas season, a young boy and his family take a whirlwind
road trip across the United States, visiting relatives from Alaska to Maine.
    ISBN 978-0-310-71588-7 (hardcover)
    [1. Christmas—Fiction. 2. Family life—Fiction. 3. Christian life—Fiction. 4.
Automobile travel—Fiction.] I. Noiset, Michele, ill. II. Title. III. Title: Seventeen
Christmases.
    PZ8.3.M179Aaj 2003
    [E]—dc22   2009008859

All Scripture quotations, unless otherwise indicated, are taken from the Holy Bible, *New International Version*®, *NIV*®. Copyright © 1973, 1978, 1984 by Biblica, Inc.™ Used by permission of Zondervan. All rights reserved worldwide.

Editor: Barbara Herndon
Art direction & design: Kris Nelson and Matthew Van Zomeren

Printed in China

10 11 12 13 14 15 /LPC/ 6 5 4 3 2 1

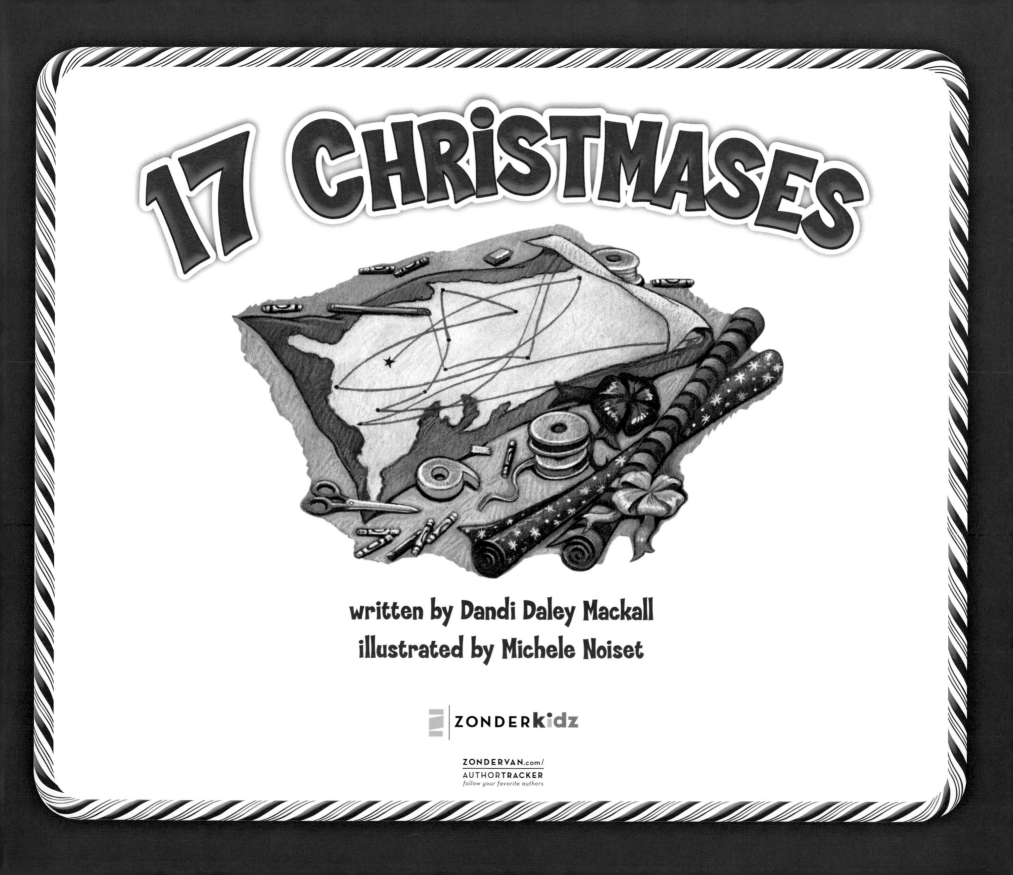

17 CHRISTMASES

written by Dandi Daley Mackall

illustrated by Michele Noiset

ZONDERkidz

ZONDERVAN.com/
AUTHORTRACKER
follow your favorite authors

Seventeen Christmases all in a row!

Get packing!

Get cracking!

Get ready to go!

With all kinds of kinfolk we really must see,

We're wrapping

And mapping

And ready to flee!

But it's weeks before Christmas . . . at least two or three.

... and to Grandma Kincaid.

We don't drink hot chocolate; we toast lemonade.

We don't "Deck the Halls," but we deck the deck bright,

Pretending we're wise men who followed the light

That guided the way that miraculous night.

Then we head out for . . .

North Carolina

In North Carolina we join in the search

For Cousin Ben's costume—he needs it for church.

I dress as a shepherd, and Ben is a sheep.

We rush to the stable. Then softly I creep ...

Right there in the manger the baby's asleep!

Then we drive up to cold . . .

We reach Colorado to see Uncle Zeke,

Who lives in a cabin on top of Pikes Peak.

We build us a snowman—it looks like Aunt Jo—

Then fall to the ground and make angels of snow.

Three Christmases down, and just fourteen to go!

Now we're off to my aunt's ranch in . . .

Texas

It's Christmas in Texas with Dad's sister Sue.

I stop counting cousins at seventy-two.

We dive in headfirst for our Christmas Eve swim,

And listen to music from Great-Uncle Jim.

I wonder if Jesus would like this old hymn.

Then we drive to my gran's in . . .

Missouri

In Missouri my granny serves turkey and ham,
Potatoes,
tomatoes,
and biscuits with jam.
We all clean our plates 'til we're very well fed,
Then snuggle up close while the Bible is read.
(We fit fourteen children in only one bed!)

Then head for the hills of ....

Ohio

In Ohio my mother hugs Grandpappy Pete,

Who calls in the neighbors who live on his street.

Then other folks join us. We sing door to door,

A choir of one hundred or possibly more.

I never got chills just from singing before.

Then it's time for Great-Grandpa's in . . .

Philly

I love Pennsylvania! We chop down our tree,

And carry it home, my great-grandpa and me.

Our tree's way too big, but we push and we shove.

Great-Gramps waves his hand toward the bright stars above

And tells me that Christmas is proof of God's love.

Then we pack up to see New York City.

Washington

We start driving east, but my mom hollers, "Wait!
We can't forget Peg back in Washington State."
So we backtrack a bit without any debate
And celebrate Christmas at Peggy's estate.
This Christmas, I'm thinking,
must be number eight.

Then we drive back to friends in . . .

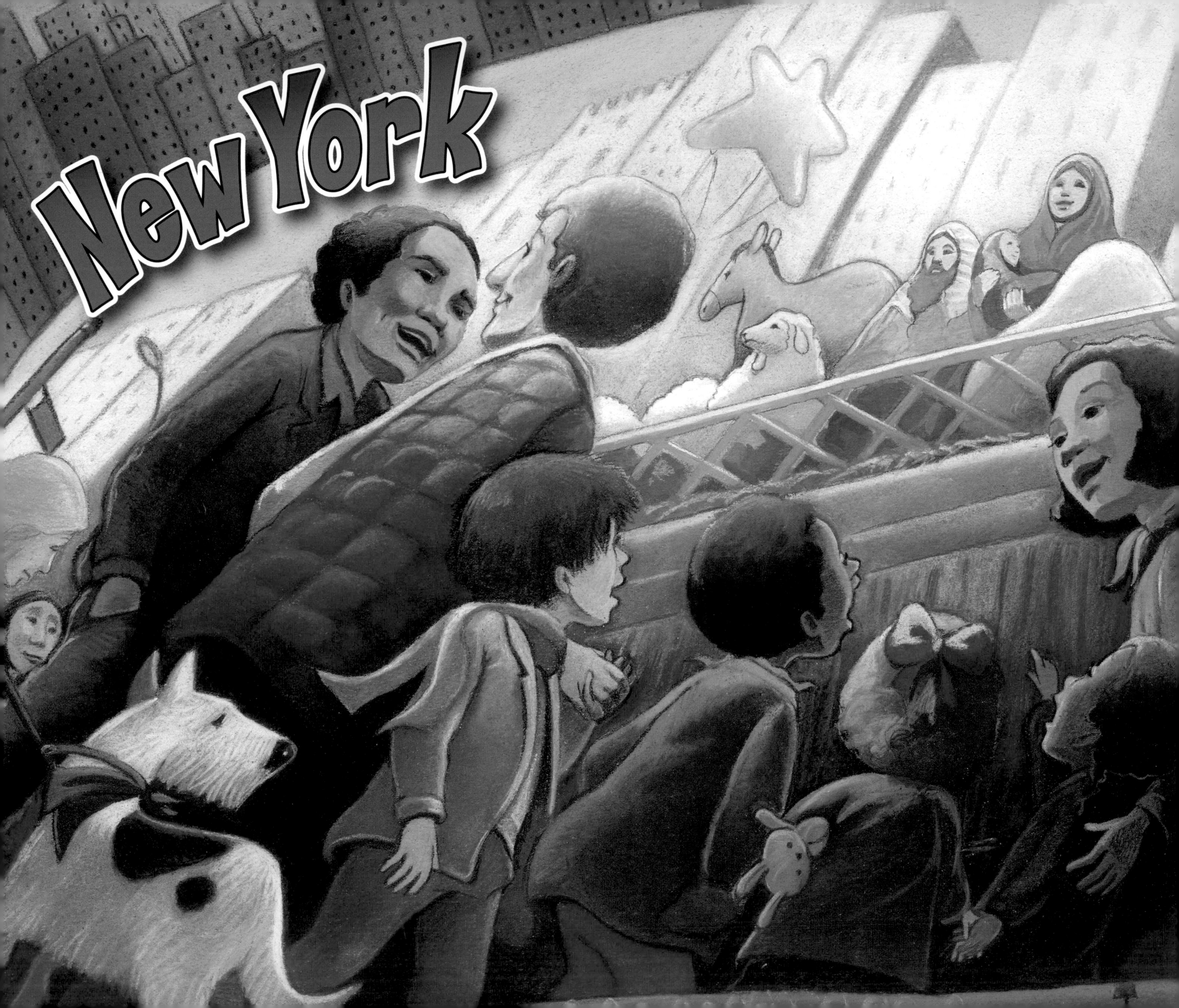
New York

New Yorkers are noisy, and Christmas is loud.

We shop in the city, get lost in the crowd.

We see a parade and enjoy decorations

And hear "Merry Christmas" in seven translations.

We pray that Christ's love spreads to all of the nations!

Then off to the folks in . . . .

Chicago

In the heart of Chicago my great-grandma Kate
Has mistletoe dangling and lying in wait.
I try to dodge kisses but get nowhere fast.
I sit by Great-Grandma, who's having a blast
And telling us stories of Christmases past.
Then we bundle up good for Alaska.

Alaska

Montana

Indiana

Maine

Louisiana

Nebraska

We have a nice Christmas with kin in Alaska,

Then drop in to visit our friends in Nebraska.

We bake hot cross buns down in south Indiana

And cook up some pralines in Ol' Louisiana.

My uncle's in Maine, and my aunt's in Montana.

Then we pile in the car one last time.

**Back home to Kentucky —
the last is the best.**

It's way past December, but still, I feel blessed.

Our Christmas tree's dry. All the needles are brown.

The fruitcake is moldy. Our stockings are down.

And Jesus is here in my very own town.

So I hum "Happy Birthday to You."

I think of the Savior and climb into bed,

While visions of Christmases dance in my head.

I thank God for Jesus and family galore,

For seventeen Christmases—never a chore.

And since I'm just eight and my sister is four...

They tell us that someday, we'll have even more!